Carol Carrick

·Valentine·

Illustrated by Paddy Bouma

Clarion Books ◆ New York

Clarion Books
a Houghton Mifflin Company imprint
215 Park Avenue South, New York, NY 10003
Text copyright © 1995 by Carol Carrick
Illustrations copyright © 1995 by Paddy Bouma

The illustrations for this book were executed in watercolor
on Fabriano cold-press watercolor paper.
The text was set in 14/18-point Garamond.

Printed in the USA.

Library of Congress Cataloging-in-Publication Data

Carrick, Carol.
Valentine / by Carol Carrick ; illustrated by Paddy Bouma.
p.   cm.
Summary: While waiting for her mother to come home from work
on Valentine's Day, Heather helps her grandmother rescue
a newborn lamb and bake a special cookie.
ISBN 0-395-66554-X   PA ISBN 0-618-05151-1
[1. Sheep—Fiction. 2. Valentine's Day—Fiction. 3. Grandmothers—Fiction.
4. Mothers and daughters—Fiction.]
I. Bouma, Paddy, ill.   II. Title.
PZ7.C2344Val   1995
[E]—dc20   94-35911
                CIP
                AC

WOZ   10   9

For Heather and Noemi
—*C.C.*

For Elizabeth
—*P.B.*

It was still dark when Mama put on her coat and hugged Heather good-bye. Mama worked in an office.

Heather held on extra tight to her mother. "Don't go," she said. "It's Valentine's Day."

Mama gave her a kiss. "It's still a work day for me," she said.

"Why do you always have to go to work?" said Heather. "I don't want you to go."

"I'm sorry," said Mama. "I would rather stay home with you."

Heather and Mama were living with Grandma. Heather felt sad as she watched Mama drive down the road. It would be dark again before her mother came home. She held her blanket against her face. It smelled like oatmeal and like Mama.

"Such a sad face on this special day!" said Grandma. "Help me make cookie valentines."

Grandma mixed butter and sugar. She added flour to make a soft dough. It felt like the clay Heather played with when she went to day care.

Grandma let Heather roll out the dough. When it was flat, they cut out cookies that looked just like Grandma's animals—chickens, cats, and sheep. Then they cut out a heart cookie for Mama's valentine.

"Can we eat one now?" asked Heather.

"No," said Grandma. "They have to bake first."

Heather sighed. She always had to wait. Wait for Valentine's Day. Wait for cookies to bake. Wait for Mama to come home.

Grandma put the first two pans in the oven. "Now! Shall we make a quick check to see how Clover is doing?" Clover was Grandma's favorite sheep.

Grandma went out to the pen where the sheep was waiting to
have her lambs. Heather followed slowly, dragging her blanket.

"Heather, come here!" Grandma sounded excited. "Clover had her babies. Two of them!" Already, the newborn lambs were on their feet and getting milk from their mother.

Heather peeked in at them. "Grandma, look! There's one more."
Behind Clover lay another little lamb. Heather reached through
the fencing to touch him. He felt stiff and cold. And he didn't
move. Something was very wrong.
"Poor little thing," said Grandma.

Heather clutched her blanket. "Is he dead?" she asked in a small voice.

Grandma picked up the lamb. She held him next to her cheek, the way Heather was holding her blanket. "I think I can feel his breath," she said. "Let's take him inside where it's warm."

Grandma filled the kitchen sink with water and put the lamb
in the warm bath. She held his head up so he could breathe.

"Are you washing him because he's dirty?" asked Heather.

"No, dear, I'm trying to get him warm. Bring me a towel from
the bathroom."

Heather hurried to get him her own towel.

Grandma lifted the lamb from the sink and wrapped him in the towel, but he still didn't move.

"Grandma! The cookies! I can smell them," said Heather.

"Heavens!" said Grandma. "I forgot. Good thing I have you to help me." She handed the lamb to Heather.

"Here," Grandma said. "Sit with the lamb by the stove while I rescue the cookies. I hope they haven't burned."

Grandma took out the pans. Heather could see that the cookies were too brown around the edges.

"I think they're tastier that way," said Grandma, but Heather didn't care about cookies now. She looked at the little lamb in her arms. His eyes were still closed and he didn't move.

"Grandma, I don't want the lamb to die," Heather said, and she began to cry.

Grandmother opened up the towel. The lamb's wet hair stuck to his wrinkled skin. Grandmother put her hand behind the lamb's front leg. She took Heather's hand and laid it on the same place. Heather could feel his heartbeat, just barely.

Grandma brought Mama's hair dryer from the bathroom and rubbed the lamb dry in the warm air.

The lamb made the smallest little sound and his head moved.

Heather smiled.

"Can you hold him," Grandma said, "while I fix him some milk?"
Heather cradled the little lamb in her lap. "There, there," she
said, patting him the way Mama patted Heather when she was
hurt. "There, there." Then she covered him with her blanket. The
blanket always made *her* feel better.

Grandma filled one of Heather's old baby bottles with warm milk. She pushed the nipple into the lamb's mouth. His lips moved. He began sucking noisily, pulling at the bottle with his mouth. Under Heather's blanket, the lamb's tail wagged. That made Heather laugh.

When the milk was gone, the lamb lifted its head and made a bleating sound, "M-a-a m-a-a-a." He began to struggle.

"He's looking for his mother," said Grandma.

"Will you put him back in the barn?" asked Heather. She didn't want him to go.

"Not today," said Grandmother. "We'll have to go on feeding him with a bottle. His mother has two other lambs to feed, and she's doing the best she can."

Heather was glad. "There, there, lamb," she said. "I'll take care of you."

Soon the lamb was asleep in the laundry basket.

Grandma put the rest of the cookies in the oven. One of them was the heart-shaped cookie for Mama.

When Mama came home, Heather showed her the lamb. That was when she knew what to call him. "His name is Valentine," she told Mama.

"He needs me," Heather said proudly. "His mother can't take care of him."

Then Heather showed Mama the cookie cats, and the chickens, and the little sheep that looked like Grandma's.

"I made this heart for you," said Heather, "because I love you."

"And I love you, too," said Mama.

"M-a-a," called Valentine, lifting his head.